This edition published in 1994 by
SMITHMARK Publishers Inc.,
16 East 32nd Street, New York,
NY 10016.

SMITHMARK books are available for bulk purchase for
sales promotion and premium use. For details write or call
the manager of special sales, SMITHMARK Publishers Inc.,
16 East 32nd Street, New York,
NY 10016; (212) 532-6600.

Produced by Brompton Books Inc.
15 Sherwood Place
Greenwich, CT 06830

ISBN 0-8317-1521-9

Printed in Hong Kong

10 9 8 7 6 5 4 3 2 1

"'VAN GOOL'S'"

The Night before Christmas

and The Twelve Days of Christmas

SMITHMARK

'Twas the night before Christmas, when all through the house
Not a creature was stirring, not even a mouse.

The stockings were hung by the chimney with care,
In hopes that St. Nicholas soon would be there.

The children were nestled all snug in their beds,
While visions of sugarplums danced in their heads.

And Mama in her kerchief, and I in my cap,
Had just settled down for a long winter's nap –

When out on the lawn there arose such a clatter,
I sprang from my bed to see what was the matter.

Away to the window I flew like a flash,
Tore open the shutters and threw up the sash.

The moon on the breast of the new-fallen snow
Gave a luster of midday to objects below.

When, what to my wondering eyes should appear,
But a miniature sleigh and eight tiny reindeer –

With a little old driver so lively and quick,
I knew in a moment it must be St. Nick.

More rapid than eagles his coursers they came,
And he whistled, and shouted, and called them by name –

"Now, Dasher! Now, Dancer! Now, Prancer and Vixen!
On, Comet! On, Cupid! On, Donner and Blitzen!

To the top of the porch,
to the top of the wall!
Now, dash away! Dash away!
Dash away all!''

As dry leaves that before the wild hurricane fly,
When they meet with an obstacle, mount to the sky,

So up to the housetop the coursers they flew,
With the sleigh full of toys – and St. Nicholas, too.

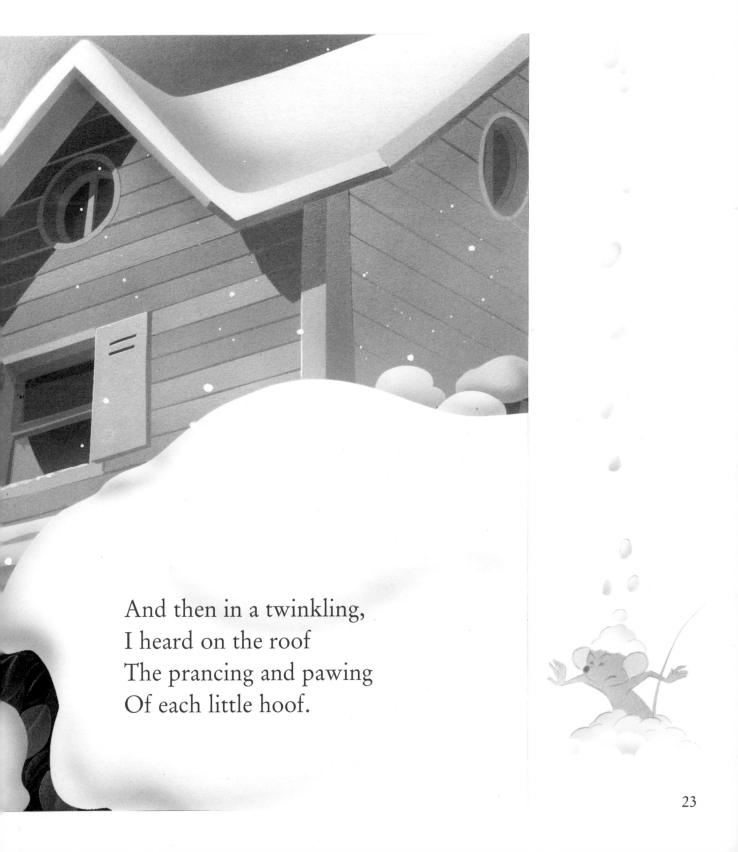

And then in a twinkling,
I heard on the roof
The prancing and pawing
Of each little hoof.

As I drew in my head, and was turning around . . .
Down the chimney St. Nicholas came with a bound!

He was dressed all in fur from his head to his foot,
And his clothes were all tarnished with ashes and soot.

A bundle of toys he had flung on his back,
And he looked like a peddler just opening his pack.
His eyes – how they twinkled! His dimples – how merry!
His cheeks were like roses, his nose like a cherry!

His droll little mouth was drawn up like a bow,
And the beard on his chin was as white as the snow!
The stump of a pipe he held tight in his teeth,
And the smoke it encircled his head like a wreath.

He had a broad face and a little round belly
That shook when he laughed like a bowl full of jelly.

He was chubby and plump – a right jolly old elf,
And I laughed when I saw him, in spite of myself!
A wink of his eye and a twist of his head,
Soon gave me to know I had nothing to dread.

He spoke not a word, but went straight to his work,
And filled all the stockings – then turned with a jerk,

And laying his finger aside of his nose,
And giving a nod, up the chimney he rose!

He sprang to his sleigh, to his team gave a whistle,
And away they all flew like the down of a thistle.

But I heard him exclaim
as he drove out of sight,

"Merry Christmas to all
and to all a Good Night!"

The Twelve Days of Christmas

On the first day of Christmas,
My true love sent to me
A partridge in a pear tree.

On the second day of Christmas,
My true love sent to me
Two turtle doves, and
A partridge in a pear tree.

On the third day of Christmas,
My true love sent to me
Three French hens,
Two turtle doves, and
A partridge in a pear tree.

On the fourth day of Christmas,
My true love sent to me
Four calling birds,
Three French hens,
Two turtle doves, and
A partridge in a pear tree.

On the fifth day of Christmas,
My true love sent to me
Five gold rings;
Four calling birds,
Three French hens,
Two turtle doves, and
A partridge in a pear tree.

On the sixth day of Christmas,
My true love sent to me
Six geese a-laying,
Five gold rings;
Four calling birds,
Three French hens,
Two turtle doves, and
A partridge in a pear tree.

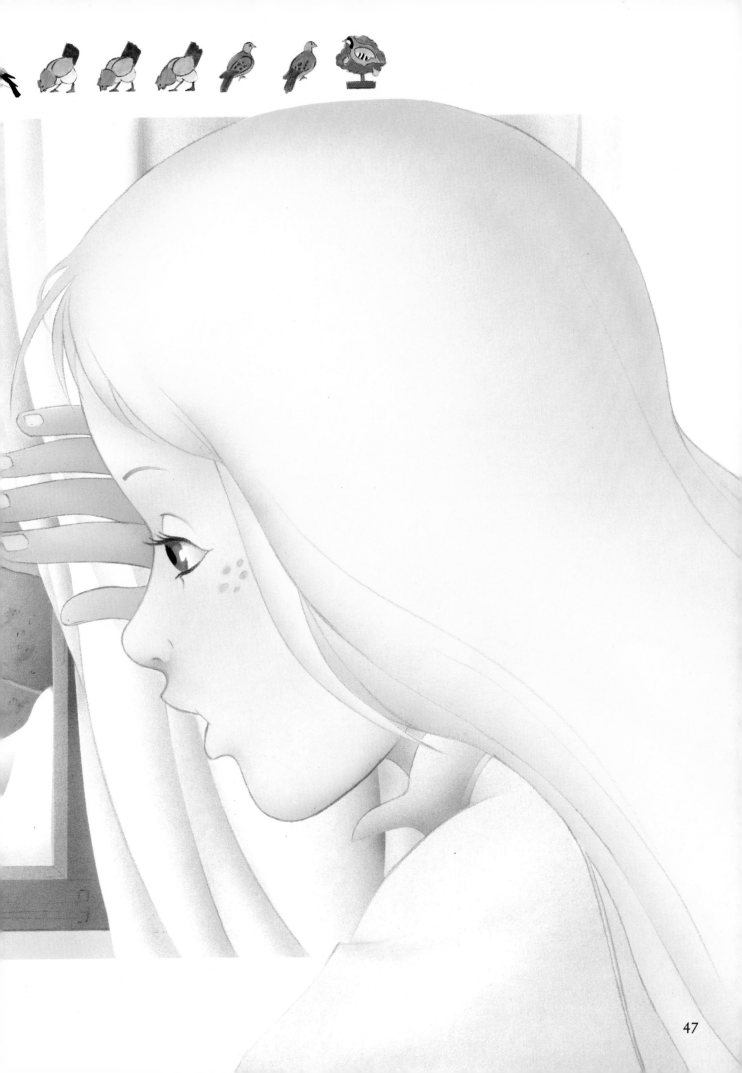

48

On the seventh day of Christmas,
My true love sent to me
Seven swans a-swimming,
Six geese a-laying,
Five gold rings;
Four calling birds,
Three French hens,
Two turtle doves, and
A partridge in a pear tree.

On the eighth day of Christmas,
My true love sent to me
Eight maids a-milking,
Seven swans a-swimming,
Six geese a-laying,
Five gold rings;
Four calling birds,
Three French hens,
Two turtle doves, and
A partridge in a pear tree.

On the ninth day of Christmas,
My true love sent to me
Nine drummers drumming,
Eight maids a-milking,
Seven swans a-swimming,
Six geese a-laying,
Five gold rings;
Four calling birds,
Three French hens,
Two turtle doves, and
A partridge in a pear tree.

On the tenth day of Christmas,
My true love sent to me
Ten pipers piping,
Nine drummers drumming,
Eight maids a-milking,
Seven swans a-swimming,
Six geese a-laying,
Five gold rings;
Four calling birds,
Three French hens,
Two turtle doves, and
A partridge in a pear tree.

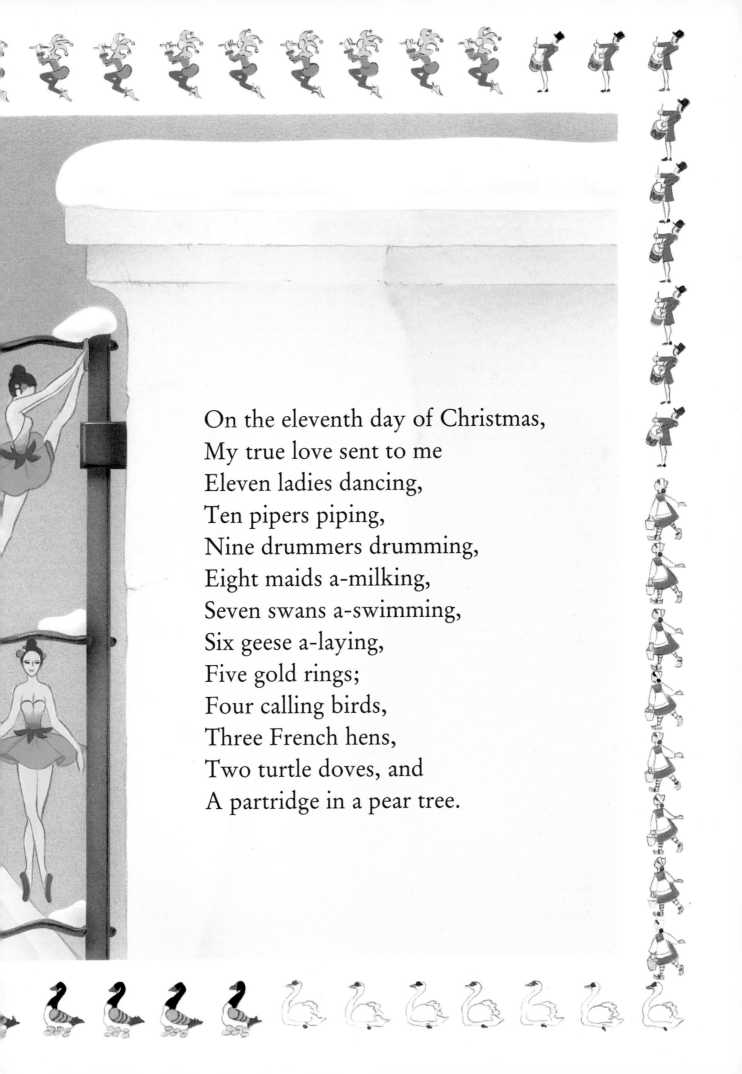

On the eleventh day of Christmas,
My true love sent to me
Eleven ladies dancing,
Ten pipers piping,
Nine drummers drumming,
Eight maids a-milking,
Seven swans a-swimming,
Six geese a-laying,
Five gold rings;
Four calling birds,
Three French hens,
Two turtle doves, and
A partridge in a pear tree.

On the twelfth day of Christmas,
My true love sent to me
Twelve lords a-leaping,
Eleven ladies dancing,
Ten pipers piping,
Nine drummers drumming,
Eight maids a-milking,
Seven swans a-swimming,
Six geese a-laying,
Five gold rings;
Four calling birds,
Three French hens,
Two turtle doves, and . . .

A partridge in a pear tree.